A Porcupine Named Fluffy

Fluffy

Helen Lester

Illustrated by Lynn Munsinger

Houghton Mifflin Harcourt
Boston   New York   2013

For more information on the importance of being true to yourself and to download a free version of this story, visit www.hmhbooks.com/freedownloads/.

Access code: beyourself

HMH Books is an imprint of Houghton Mifflin Harcourt Publishing Company.

www.hmhbooks.com

The text of this book is set in Adobe Garamond Pro.

Library of Congress Cataloging-in-Publication Control Number 85-24820

ISBN 978-0-544-00319-4
Manufactured in China
SCP 10 9 8 7 6 5 4 3 2 1
4500406235

When Mr. and Mrs. Porcupine had
their first child, they were delighted.
Now he needed a name.

Should they call him Spike?
No. Spike was too common.

Should they call him Lance?
No. Lance sounded too fierce.
Should they call him Needleroozer?
No. Needleroozer was too long.
Prickles? Pokey? Quillian?
Then together they had an idea.
"Let's call him Fluffy.
It's such a pretty name.
Fluffy!"

But soon there came a time when Fluffy began to doubt that he was fluffy.

He first became suspicious when he backed into
a door and stuck fast.
That was not a fluffy thing to do.

He was even more convinced when he accidentally
slept on his back and poked holes in the mattress.
A very unfluffy thing to do.

When he tried to carry an umbrella he
knew the truth without a doubt.

Fluffy definitely wasn't.

So he decided to become fluffier.
"Clouds are fluffy," he thought. "I'll be a cloud."

But he couldn't stay up.

"I know. Pillows are fluffy!" he said. "I'll be a pillow."
But when his mother sat on him,
she was not pleased.

He tried soaking in a bubble bath for
forty-five minutes, but he did not become fluffy.
He became soggy.

He tried whipped cream.
He put a little on each quill. It was not easy,
and it took more than half a day.

But this did not make Fluffy fluffy.
"They should have named me Gooey," he sighed.

He ate a lot of fluffy marshmallows.

He rolled in shaving cream
and feathers.

He even tried to become a bunny.

But the truth remained.
Fluffy wasn't.

One afternoon Fluffy set out for a walk,
trying to think of ways to become fluffy.

Before long he met a very large rhinoceros.

"Grrrr!" said the rhinoceros. "I'm going
to give you a rough time."
Fluffy didn't know what a rough time was,
but he didn't like the sound of it at all.
"What is your name, small prickly thing?"
asked the rhinoceros unkindly.
"Fluffy," said Fluffy.

The rhinoceros smiled.
He giggled.
Then he laughed out loud.
He rolled on the ground.
He jiggled and slapped his knees.
He roared with laughter.

"A porcupine named Fluffy!" howled the rhinoceros.

Fluffy was embarrassed, but he tried to be polite.
"And what is *your* name?" he inquired.

"H . . . I can't say it," giggled the rhinoceros.
"Hubert?" suggested Fluffy.

H . . . H . . . H . . . oh help, I just can't say it, I'm laughing so hard," said the rhinoceros. "Harold? Or maybe Herman?" asked Fluffy. "No," gasped the rhinoceros. "It's H . . . H . . . H . . . H . . . H . . .

. . . HIPPO."

Hippo.

A rhinoceros named Hippo.

Fluffy smiled.

He giggled.

Then he laughed out loud.

He jiggled and slapped his knees.

He howled with laughter.

"A rhinoceros named Hippo!" Fluffy cried.

A porcupine named Fluffy.
A rhinoceros named Hippo.
It was almost more than they could bear.
Hippo and Fluffy rolled on the ground giggling and laughing
until tears came to their eyes.

At last they lay exhausted on the ground.
From that time on they were the best of friends.

And Fluffy didn't mind being Fluffy anymore —
even though he wasn't.